Thomas

AND THE PONY

by Christopher Awdry

illustrated by Ken Stott

First published in Great Britain in this edition 1997
by Reed Books Children's Publishing
Michelin House, 81 Fulham Road, London SW3 6RB
and Auckland and Melbourne

Copyright © Reed International Books Ltd 1993
All publishing rights Reed International Books Ltd
All television and merchandising rights licensed by
Reed International Books Ltd to
Britt Allcroft (Thomas) Ltd, exclusively, worldwide

ISBN 0 7497 3044 7

1 3 5 7 9 10 8 6 4 2

Printed in Great Britain

Thomas was waiting at the station for the guard to blow his whistle and wave his flag. He saw Becky and her mother come onto the platform.

Thomas knew Becky well. He often saw her riding her pony, Barnaby, as he puffed past the farm where she lived.

Thomas knew there was to be a Pony Show in Fox's Field. "I wish I could see it," he thought. "Becky is sure to be there riding Barnaby."

The day of the Pony Show was beautiful and sunny.
Thomas saw men preparing for the show as he
passed Fox's Field.

Thomas was humming happily as he ran along the rails.
But as he came round a curve in the line, he saw a
horsebox standing on the road.

Becky stood beside the horsebox looking worried.
Her father was bending down beside the front wheels.

"It looks as if they have broken down," said Thomas' driver. "Poor Becky. She will be disappointed if she has to miss the show."

The Stationmaster was waiting for Thomas at the next station.
"Becky was on her way to the Pony Show when her horsebox
broke down," he told Thomas' driver.

"The Fat Controller has asked if Thomas will take Barnaby, Becky and her mother to the Show. Her father will wait for the breakdown lorry."

A horsebox was coupled to Clarabel and the porter opened the doors. The ticket collector shook his head as the pony was led onto the platform. "Most unusual," he said.

Becky and her mother walked Barnaby up the ramp
and when the pony was safely shut in the stall, they
sat down at the back and Thomas set off again.

Fox's Field was near the next station. Quickly, Becky led Barnaby out of the horsebox and trotted him to the starting point.

Thomas was glad to see she was smiling again.
As she reached the starting point her name was
called out. She was only just in time.

While Thomas watched, Barnaby jumped a clear round.
Everyone clapped and Thomas whistled excitedly:
"Peep pip pip peeeeeeep."

But Thomas had to go before the results were announced.
"I wonder if Becky will get a prize?" he kept saying.
"I do hope so."

The next day, Becky and Barnaby were waiting for him at the station. Barnaby was wearing a big red rosette, and Becky had brought a yellow one for Thomas.

"Thank you, Thomas," she said happily. "We would never have won without you."
Thomas was happy too.